THE AMISH HOSTAGE

Rachel Yoder-May

ISBN-10: 1519760418
ISBN-13: 978-1519760418

More Info

Sign up to get a mail when I publish a new Amish Romance.

http://amishromance.xyz/info/

Summary

Amish Romance and Suspense

Katie Zook, a headstrong Amish girl, has a crush on the shy Samuel Lapp and hopes to break the ice between them. When they are both taken hostage by a desperate robber, Katie can't just keep quiet and allow things to happen. Now the robber gives her an ultimatum: Get rid of the police if she and Samuel want to live.

CHAPTER 1

Katie stared as hypnotized on the TV-screen on the wall. The sound was off, but it didn't matter. It was fascinating to watch Englischers doing their stuff in a world so far from hers.

Reluctantly, she turned away. She was here to shop, not to watch TV.

She picked up a bottle of dark molasses and a bag of flour. She thought of the shoo fly pie her mother had promised to make this afternoon, and she could almost smell and taste it.

Katie consulted her shopping list. There was only one item left on it, and she headed towards the fresh fruit and grabbed a bag of oranges.

Oh, bananas. They looked delicious. Her mother hadn't told her to get any, but would she mind if she bought a couple? Certainly not.

But what was that?

Three rows from her, she caught sight of something far more interesting than moving pictures and fruit.

Samuel Lapp. She would have recognized his tall frame anywhere.

Her heart beat harder and louder and blood rushed to her cheeks. Talk about luck. Meeting him here was an excellent opportunity.

So he's never offered to drive her home from singing? That wouldn't matter. She was on foot - barefooted - and he surely wouldn't deny her plea for a buggy ride home.

She straightened up, smoothed a few folds on her skirt, checked her bonnet and went straight in his direction.

She had her eyes fixed on him, when he looked up, and their gazes crossed. It was like getting an electric bolt that hit her.

Samuel wasn't exactly handsome, but he had the most beautiful and honest blue eyes. Deep blue. Katie would love to dive into his eyes and drown in them.

She saluted him, and he waved back.

Oh, no, you're not getting off the hook that easy, young man.

Katie kept approaching him, and Samuel seemed to study the floor. He didn't get closer, but he didn't exactly flee, either.

Why was he so shy? Or maybe he wasn't interested in her?

There was only one way to find out.

"Hi Samuel. Are you out shopping?" Ouch, she could have kicked herself for that question. What else would he be doing in the grocery store?

"Yes, Mem needed a few things we didn't have in our garden."

Katie craned her neck to look into his shopping basket. It contained milk, butter and cream. "If you like, we can swop groceries? We have a cow on our farm, but not that many vegetables."

"Maybe. I'll ask at home."

He wasn't exactly easy to strike up a conversation with. What more could they talk about? She thought for a moment.

"Are you going to the singing next Sunday?"

He nodded and fumbled with the handles of the basked. "Yeah. I plan to."

Why didn't he ask if she was going?

Katie bit her lip. A part of her felt like screaming. Instead, she smiled. She had a plan.

"Ouch, my basket is really heavy. All the grocery I need to carry home. And unfortunately," she wriggled her bare feet, "I'm on foot."

Samuel gazed at her feet but didn't say anything.

"Did you drive your buggy here?"

"Yes, I always do."

Good. He would have to let her drive home with her. Denying her help would be rude, and Samuel would never be rude. If only she could pick the right words.

"Would you mind driv—"

"HELP! Help!"

The screams came from the area near the cash register

and Samuel and Katie both turned towards the sound.

Katie froze on the spot and widened her eyes.

She'd known the manager of the store, Richard Bradley, all her life. He was a man in his fifties, almost bald and always sweaty, wearing a white coat over his clothes, summer as well as winter.

Whether the shop was packed with customers or quiet like today, he was invariably calm and smiling, humming behind his counter.

Today was different.

Bradley was standing with his back to the wall, both hands in the air.

In front of him was a man, she'd never seen before.

He was taller than her, but not much. Brown hair, a little too long for an Englischer. He was wearing clean, but worn clothes, blue jeans and a green tee shirt, and he seemed to have bare feet in sneakers.

He had his back turned towards her, so she couldn't see his face, but she could see his hand and what it was holding.

He pointed a gun directly at the manager's chest.

CHAPTER 2

"You can't do that!"

Katie rushed towards the robber and poked his shoulder. That man was doing something awful.

"Huh?"

The robber faced her. He had a kind face, but looked tired. He had no facial hair, not even stubbles.

"It's a sin."

"Are you crazy, girl?"

"No, but look at the manager. You've frightened him. You shouldn't do that."

"What the… Are you totally wacko?" He widened his eyes.

"I'm completely sane, but you're doing something

horrible. What's your name?"

"Thomas." The robber bit his lib as if regretting that he answered her.

"Good, Thomas. I'm Katie. Now put down your gun and leave the store. Nobody will tell anyone about what you did, but you have to stop now."

Bradley made a slight move and bend over the counter. Was he about to faint?

Thomas turned towards him. "What did you just do? Did you just do something?" He waved his gun in front of his face.

The manager went pale and bend over again. This time Katie was certain that he was going to pass out. His legs seemed to cross out beneath him and he slid under the desk.

A metallic sound coming from the side of the store grabbed her attention, and she turned towards it.

The doors close shut.

How could they do that? Were there some kind of button the manager could use to remote control the doors?

Katie was used to doors you opened and closed with your hand, but these ones opened when a customer approached it either from the inside of the store or the outside.

It was possible that the manager had closed them from the inside.

Thomas jumped. He'd seen it too.

"What did you do?" He bend over the counter to look down at the manager who squatted on the floor. He held his head in his hands and his whole body was shaking.

Then Katie heard them. Faint to begin with, then louder as they came closer. Sirens from police cars.

"You idiot!" Thomas was jumping up and down now. "You pushed a silent alarm, didn't you? Well, it's not going to do you any good."

He turned around facing Katie, Samuel and two other - pale - customers.

"Listen very carefully. All of you. Sit down quietly, and nothing will happen to you. But if you try anything smart I will kill you. Now! Sit down!"

The last two orders sounded like gunshots in the air.

Katie ran over to Samuel, and they both sat down. The two other customers were already seated.

"Listen."

Thomas hadn't finished his speech. "Nobody will leave this store, before the police has moved away and I have the money I came for. Is that understood?"

CHAPTER 3

Katie frowned.

From her place on the floor, she could see the profiles of the two Englischers, who happened to shop in the store when Thomas held up the manager.

They were both nodding and confirming that they'd understood Thomas' words. They both looked scared.

She turned towards Samuel. He didn't move, but he seemed calm.

How lucky they were to have a strong faith.

Thomas looked satisfied with the two nods. He turned towards Bradley again. "Get up. You can stop pretending to have fainted now. I know what you did."

The manager stood up, but he was even paler than before. His eyes looked black in contrast to his bluish white face.

May Gotte protect me.

Katie stood up and walked towards the robber. Her bare feet made no sound on the floor, and she counted to three while inhaling and exhaling. Easy now. Don't scare him.

Then she stood next to him. She smiled. "Thomas?"

He turned towards her and widened his eyes. He didn't look like a bad man. Why was he doing this?

Thomas was sweating now. He wiped away a drop that threatened to run into his left eye, and she could smell him. It wasn't old, dirty sweat, but a fresh, salty scent.

"Thomas, listen to your heart. Release us all. Let us go."

He opened his mouth, but no sound came out. He closed it again and narrowed his eyes. Then he shook his head.

His hand with the gun didn't move. It still pointed at the manager.

"Shut up, girl."

"My name is Katie."

"I don't care," he yelled. "Shut up, Kay-tee, and go and sit down."

Why wouldn't he listen?

Katie couldn't explain her feelings, but she knew somehow that Thomas wasn't a bad man. He was just desperate and doing something wrong right now. If only she could reach him and make him see it.

"Sit!" He yelled again, and she sat down for his feet.

With a sigh, he turned towards the manager again. Good. So he didn't consider her dangerous.

More police cars were gathering outside. They had shut down their sirens, but flashing blue and red lights showed their presence and lit up the walls in the shop.

How would this end? Would they storm the shop and arrest the robber? Would he shoot at them, maybe kill somebody?

Footsteps. Right behind her. She twisted her neck and saw Samuel approaching her. He looked calm. She smiled. So he was shy, and yet strong inside. He would be a gut mann. Her heart was right.

"Hi," he said and smiled a little.

"Hi." She felt her heart go boom-boom again and her smile must have covered most of her face.

He sat down beside her and grabbed her hand. He squeezed it. She squeezed back.

Thomas turned his head, stared at them for a few seconds, but said nothing. Then he shook his head and focused on the manager again.

"Hand me the money."

The manager opened the cash register and took up a bundle of notes. He handed them over to the robber.

"There must be more in there."

The manager almost turned green. "No… That's it. Only those and… and checks."

"That's not enough," he said so low that Katie wasn't even sure these were the words.

Enough for what?

"You should give him his money back. Stealing is a sin." She rose and squatted instead of sitting on the floor. She'd been uncomfortable long enough and her legs slept.

"Sin? What do you call sin? Against your God? I need money and nobody cares. Isn't that a sin, too?"

Thomas' face was red and he looked as if he was ready to explode.

"Not just against God. Also against your fellow man. You're hurting three persons when you steal. God, your neighbor and yourself."

"Oh, stop it! Shut up now. If you really want to talk, then go and talk to the police. Ask them to leave. Yes, ask them to leave now, or…" He stopped. Widened his eyes, looked at the gun in his hand, and then at her. "Or I'll kill you."

CHAPTER 4

"That would be an even bigger sin." Katie didn't lower her gaze. She looked right into Thomas' brown eyes, until he closed them and looked away. He pursed his lips and took a deep breath.

"Listen, Thomas—"

"Look!" Samuel interrupted her and pointed at something outside. "The press is here. It's Jones." He turned towards Katie. "She interviewed you too last year, didn't she?"

Katie squeezed her eyes to study the woman outside. She was in her thirties, obese, clad in black and wore a scarf on her head. Yes, it looked like Jones who'd made a transmission about Amish youngsters last year. She'd been very interested in learning about their rumspringa and how far they were willing to go to test the outside world. The world of the Englischers.

Jones squatted in front of the store and shielded her eyes with her hand to look in. Then she crossed gazes with Katie and waved. Katie waved back, but Jones was already on her way back to a huge van.

"We're on TV." Samuel pointed towards the TV that was still running.

"Turn up the sound," Thomas said and waved the gun at Bradley, who hurried to obey.

"...standing outside the store right now where a hostage situation is taking place." A man in a suit with a black tie looked directly at the camera and seemed to speak straight to his audience.

"Five people have been taken hostage by an unscrupulous armed robber. Police hopes that the robber will release the hostages. He's not known to the police, but we've found out who he is."

The camera zoomed to a newspaper article and they all saw a picture of a smiling Thomas, hugging an elder handicapped woman.

The journalist continued. "Here he is, Thomas Rees, 37-years-old, with his handicapped mother. According to this article, he sat up a charity event to collect money to help his mother to get lifesaving medicine."

The camera zoomed in on the journalist again. "We don't know how that turned out and if his actions today are a reflection of his need for money to help his mother."

He smiled to the camera.

"Stand by for more information about the hostage situation after this message from our sponsor."

Katie swallowed a lump in her throat. So Thomas wasn't doing this for his own sake. It was still a sin, of course. But done as an act of assistance for another human being, was the sin just as serious?

"What do you think?" She whispered the question to Samuel, afraid Thomas would hear them.

He pushed out his underlip. "Makes his acts more understandable, but still wrong."

"I agree with you." She would have loved to discuss this topic further, but Thomas stared at her and he didn't look happy.

The advert faded out and the journalist returned to the screen.

They all focused on the TV to learn more about their own situation.

"You're watching a direct transmission from the hostage situation in our local grocery store, where my colleague Samantha Jones has news. Right, Jones?"

The screen showed the face of a serious looking Jones with a hand-held microphone in front of her mouth.

"I'm standing outside a little farm house in the Amish village. A woman is sitting behind me on a bench. She has her face turned away from the cameras as it's against her faith to have photographies taken."

She turned around and faced a seated woman wearing the blue dress that was so typical for Amish women. She wore a white bonnet and an apron.

"Will you tell the viewers your name, madam?"

"Yes. I'm Mrs. Isaac Zook."

Katie gasped.

"Mrs. Zook, do you know where your daughter is?"

"She's in the shop, taken hostage."

Her shoulders were shaking, but you couldn't hear her crying.

The screen looked blurred to Katie and she didn't hear

the other questions Jones asked her mother.

Her chest ached.

She wasn't afraid of dying. If it was God's will that she had to go, then there was nothing she could do.

But her mother being sad for her? That was another thing.

Suddenly it mattered a lot to her to stay alive. Not for her sake, but for her mother's.

CHAPTER 5

Samuel grabbed her hand and squeezed it. Her heart skipped a beat and in spite of the conditions, it made her feel good to feel his strong hand around hers.

They had to get out of this situation. She had so much to live for, and she wanted to see her mother happy again.

She wouldn't mind Samuel courting her either. She smiled when she thought of her plan to get him to offer her a ride home. Was that really only one hour ago?

Here they were now. Five people plus a robber with a gun, locked inside a grocery store. Police outside. Waiting or doing something? She had no idea. So far they'd only arrived in their cars. What was the normal hostage procedure?

She peeked out of the big store window. The officers seemed to be standing outside their cars, two by two, just looking at the store.

Maybe somebody was supposed to give a "go" signal. She shuddered. What would happen to them if the police bursted in, armed, maybe firing towards Thomas. Would they get hit, too?

She jumped up, still holding Samuel's hand.

"You have to turn yourself in."

"What?" Thomas widened his eyes.

"They will understand. Your punishment won't be hard, because you're doing this for your mother."

Thomas lowered the gun. Until now he'd kept it pointed at the manager's chest.

His hands were hanging down his sides. Katie studied his right hand, holding the gun. His fingers were loosening their grip. She waited for the sound of the gun, dropping to the floor.

Thomas flexed his fingers a bit. Then his knuckles went white, and he raised the gun again. This time he pointed it in her direction.

Katie looked up to meet his gaze, but he was staring past her. She followed his regard. It led to her hand, clutching the hand of Samuel.

Why was he looking at their hands?

"I'm not turning myself in. I need the money. And I need the freedom to help my mother. If people had cared, they would have given at the charity. But people don't care. Only about themselves."

"The Englischers might be like that, but when one of us needs help we—"

"I don't care what you do. I only care about getting some medicine for my mother so she won't die. Understood? Now make the police go away."

She shook her head.

"So you won't help me? Yeah, why should you care about me or my mother. You don't even care for your own life. But maybe you care about this. How about you make the police go away, or I'll shoot your boyfriend here instead."

Katie sat down. Kill Samuel? Dizziness overwhelmed her and her vision blurred.

She didn't have a choice anymore. She had to make the police leave.

But could she? Would they listen to a young Amish girl?

Her stomach felt hard as a rock.

Chapter 6

"How do I contact the police? Will you let me out?"

Thomas smiled, but only with his lips. "Do you think I'm that stupid?"

"I don't think you're stupid, but they will not be able to hear me through the doors. They are made out of thick glass."

"That's your problem. Just make them go away, or..." He waved the gun in the direction of Samuel, who was still holding her hand.

She took a deep breath. This had to work. "Okay, then. I'll talk to them."

"Take this." Samuel handed her his white handkerchief.

She raised an eyebrow.

"I know you don't look like Thomas," he said. "But just in case..."

She grabbed it and crossed the floor to approach the door. As she got closer, she saw four policemen move closer to her. Hopefully they would be able to hear her and would listen.

When she stood close to the door, she formed a funnel with her hands and placed them in front of her mouth and shouted, "Go away."

All four officers shook their head.

Katie bit her lip. "You have to. He's going to kill Samuel."

Then she noticed that one of the policemen were carrying a megaphone. He raised it to his lips and shouted, "Sorry. We're not negotiating with hostage takers."

"But he'll kill him," she shouted from the top of her lungs.

"Sorry," he said, and his eyes moistened.

Then they all backed away and went back to their cars.

Katie turned, and her feet felt heavy as she walked towards Thomas again.

He had his lips pressed together, forming a narrow line. So he'd heard.

Samuel got up and in two steps he stood face to face with Thomas.

"I'm not afraid of death. But if you think it will change your situation, you're wrong. The police is not going to budge."

Thomas pointed his gun towards Samuel's head. He had to raise his hand to do so, Samuel being taller than him.

Tears were pouring out her eyes now, blurring her vision. She nearly stumbled over one of the two Englischers who were kept hostage, too. Why didn't they speak up? Sure, Thomas had a gun, but he could only point it at one person at a time, and they were five hostages in here. If somebody had the courage to do something, they could overpower him and take control.

Then she knew the answer.

They didn't do anything, because they were afraid. They didn't share her faith. Death was terrifying and not a natural course of life.

And had it helped her that she took action? No, not at all. It had only gone from bad to worse.

Now he would kill Samuel, because she spoke up?

She couldn't let that happen.

"Stop," she said, facing Thomas, capturing his attention. "Samuel had nothing to do with this. I was the one to try to make you hand yourself over to the police. I was to blame, not him. I thought I could talk to the kind and loving person inside you. But I was wrong. Take me instead. Don't kill Samuel."

Thomas stared at her with a blank look in his eyes.

"Okay," he said.

Good, he'd accepted. She wouldn't have been able to continue her life with Samuel's death on her conscience.

There was only one thing missing, and she would be able to die in peace.

"Will you allow me to say a last prayer?"

He nodded, and his adam's apple moved as if he was swallowing.

Katie kneeled down in front of Thomas. She could feel the heat from Samuel's body. He was sitting next to her. She forced herself to smile to him. Her heart skipped a beat. Samuel looked so pale.

Then she closed her eyes and folded her hands.

The movement was so familiar. This would be her last prayer, but she suddenly remembered how her mother had showed her how to fold her hands, when she was only a toddler. How her mother had kneeled down with her and said the words that formed her short prayer.

She pressed her eyes shut to exclude the sight of her mother's face and eyes. Her mother's crying eyes.

CHAPTER 7

Katie finished her prayer. She was feeling at peace, but sad because of her mother.

A clicking sound warned her that Thomas disengaged the safety of the gun. She opened her eyes.

Thomas was looking at her, his gun hanging down his side. His hand was shaking.

She felt sorry for him. He was one of the Englischers, and they didn't take care of each other, such as they did in her Gmay. An old woman would never have been left to die without medicine, no matter how much money it cost.

They would have found a way. They would all have donated what they could, and then they would have worked harder to make more money so they could keep helping.

What choice did he have?

She got up from her kneeling position and stood in front of him. At least he had to look her in her eyes when he shot her.

His blue eyes didn't seem evil. He looked sad. And shaken, somehow.

"Step back," he said.

Katie took one step back. Then Samuel stepped in front of her.

"If you shoot her, you'll have to kill me first."

Oh, no, why did he do that? She was at peace and ready to die. He didn't need to die, too.

Thomas didn't say anything. He raised his shaking hand, holding the gun.

Katie couldn't see exactly where he aimed, because her vision was blocked by Samuel.

"Pray with me, Katie." Samuel took her hand and dragged her down as he kneeled himself.

His hand was dry and calm.

Maybe he was right. They would show Thomas the

right way to behave. Not to use cowardly methods to force people to do something they were unwilling to do.

But to have faith in God and that he would look out for them and take care of their needs.

On her knees she crawled forward so she could sit next to Samuel. She reached over and took his left hand, folding her hand over his, merged her fingers into his.

His right hand held her left, and his left hand were folded in prayer with her right.

Together they lifted their spirit and prayed. She thought of her mother and with a sudden certainty she knew her mother would understand and approve of what she'd done.

This was the only way. She had to speak up like she'd done. She had to do her best to convince Thomas that he was committing a sin, and that there were other ways to solve a problem than by using violence.

If she'd kept silent, she would have shown approval of his behavior. Then she would have participated in his sin.

Yes, she'd done the right thing, and Samuel, who would have been such a good man, had approved of her acts.

She squeezed his right hand tighter, and as with one voice they both said, "Amen."

CHAPTER 8

Katie opened her eyes. She was ready now.

Thomas was in front of her. She stared right into his sneakers and blue jeans. There was no urge to look further up.

Now it would only be a question of seconds before she and Samuel would die together, hand in hand.

She took a deep breath and closed her eyes again. "Thank you God, for my life. I appreciate what you've given me and all the kind people I've been surrounded by."

Katie was ready.

"Okay, you win." Thomas almost yelled the words. Then he handed over the gun to Samuel. "Here, take it. You win."

Samuel grabbed the gun. He wasn't supposed to hold a weapon, but in this case Katie understood him. It was always more important to save lives than to follow the exact words of the Ordnung.

He held it out from his body as if it was a live snake.

"How can you be so calm at the face of death?" Thomas shook his head. His eyes were wide and dark. He swallowed.

Police would take care of him, and he knew it without doubt.

"Death is just a part of life. Why should we fear it?" Samuel spoke without fear. The shy man she knew had gone. She'd always felt that he was special and had more in him than what he showed. He looked strong and good.

"Besides, we have our faith to support us." She turned her head to face Thomas.

He was biding his lips now. "Faith… Faith doesn't give you food, rent or money."

"Are you sure? We've never lacked of anything. God provides us with what we need."

"If only that was true…"

"It is. Open your heart to the Lord, and you'll see."

He smiled. "I might. I'll hand myself over to the police now, and I guess I'll have plenty of time to study the Bible and check out your God in jail."

Katie laughed. "Who are you fooling? You have opened your heart already. Here... Before you go, give me your mother's address, and our community will take care of her needs."

Thomas blinked. "You will? After what I've done to you? I nearly... killed you."

"Yes, but you didn't. That's what counts."

Samuel finally gave up holding the gun. He squatted and put it under his foot. Then he stood again. "Katie is right. Your acts count. Not what you threatened to do, but your acts of kindness in the end. You are a good man."

"Not so sure the judge will think the same. But thank you for your kind words, young man." He turned towards the manager. "Please open the doors."

Then he addressed Samuel again. "Could I borrow that handkerchief of yours, please? I'd better make sure the police sees that I'm giving myself up so they don't shoot my head off when they enter."

Samuel gave him the handkerchief Katie had used a short while ago.

Thomas grabbed it and shook Samuel's hand. He turned towards her and bowed. "You're a stubborn woman. But you were right. Thank you."

Then he walked towards the doors, holding the white handkerchief up as a sign of peace.

Katie saw the police approach with guns in hand, grabbing him and following him into a car. She got one last glimpse of his blue eyes when the car drove away.

Samuel put his arm around her shoulder. "So it all ended well. We should get home now with our groceries."

"I haven't paid for mine."

"Neither have I. Let's go to the cash register."

They approached the manager who were standing behind the desk, still pale, but visibly relieved.

"Let's just say I owe you. Here, let me put those groceries into bags and they are on the house today. Together with this." He took two expensive looking boxes of chocolate and put them in each a bag. Then he handed them over the desk. "Here you are. You were very brave."

"Thank you." Katie smiled. She hadn't been brave. She'd just done what her heart told her to do.

Samuel thanked the manager as well, and they walked outside.

"Let me drive you home. My buggy is right over here." Samuel was no longer shy. He'd faced more dangerous situations than risking a rejection.

"Thank you. I would love to let you drive me home." Katie smiled. She'd never felt so happy before in her life.

"Oh, and before I forget. Are you coming to the singing next Sunday?"

"Of course I am," she said. He'd dared to ask. He cared.

"Good," he nodded. "Allow me to drive you home after the singing, too, will you?"

She winked. "We'll see about that. First, I have to know how well you drive. Oh, watch out, there's a stone on the road."

They both laughed.

The future looked bright for Katie. She leaned her head against his shoulder. Very bright indeed.

The End.

Word List

Aenti = aunt

Ausbund = Amish hymnal

Bruder = brother

Dat = dad

Dokder = doctor

Englischer = American, non-Amish

Gesicht = face

Gmay = community

Gotte = god

Gut = good

Kochoffe = Cook stove

Mann = man

Meedel = girl

Mem = mom

Onkel = uncle

Ordnung = the unwritten ruleset the Amish live by

Rumspringa = period of freedom for an Amish youngster, before he/she decides to join or leave the Amish

Wasser = water

My Other Amish Romance Books

Read my other sweet and clean Amish Romance books. You will find them here:

Naomi's Destiny

From the age of five, Naomi had to take care of her two younger siblings. She always strived to do her best, but now her family is threatened and there's nothing she can do.

Atlee faces problems he never imagined having at his age. His father is seriously ill, and should the worst thing happen, Atlee has to take over as head of the family.

In spite of their problems, it is instant love between Naomi and Atlee.

But they are parted by distance as well as duties.

Will the two young people be able to find true love and be together?

http://amzn.com/B011LSMSL8

Courting the Amish Widow

Amish schoolteacher Esther Miller is a 27-year-old widow without children, who gets a chance of starting a family by adopting newly-orphaned Nathan and Emily.

When a handsome stranger shows up and claims to be the father who everybody thought was dead, she is split between feeling attracted to him and not believing his story.

Now Esther has to figure out if she's fighting for the children or for her own happiness.

http://amzn.com/B0117Y5HX2

Lost in Holmes County

Sarah Miller finds herself lying on the ground outside a farm. It's dark, her head hurts, and she's lost her memory.

She's clenching a piece of paper in her hand. The note says, "Sarah, come and see me. Paul"

It's freezing cold, so she seeks help at the nearby farm, where the Amish widower Dannie Troyer lives alone.

But even though Sarah comes to love and trust

Dannie, she isn't safe on his farm, and the past threatens to catch up with her.

Will Sarah get her memory back in time to save her from whatever is haunting her?

And will her budding love for Dannie be allowed to grow and to be returned?

Read this sweet and clean Amish Romance Mystery to find out.

http://amzn.com/B016XIY5N0

Sign up to get a mail when I publish a new Amish Romance.

http://amishromance.xyz/info/

It would make me happy, if you would spend a few minutes reviewing this book on Amazon, once you've read it.

If there were things you didn't like, you're welcome to contact me directly. I'm always striving to write better books, so I love any kind of feedback.

My email is rachel@amishromance.xyz

You can also find me on Facebook on this page: http://www.facebook.com/rachelyodermay

I would love to meet you there, so please "Like" it and say "hi" :)

51044988R20029

Made in the USA
Lexington, KY
11 April 2016